MAKING MODELS

Ray Gibson
Edited by Kathy Gemmell
Designed by Non Figg

Illustrated by Raymond Turvey and David Eaton
Photographs by Amanda Heywood
Series editor: Cheryl Evans

Additional photographs by Ray Moller
With thanks to Lee Erskine, Tessa Forge,
Harry Gibson and Rachel McCulloch

Contents

Animals

Follow the steps opposite to make these clay animals. Whenever you come across words in **bold** lettering, look in the *Techniques* box to find out what you have to do.

You will need: old knife, large stone with a flat base, PVA glue, self-hardening clay, pencil, cocktail sticks (2 cut in half), garlic press, small beads, poster paints, newspapers.

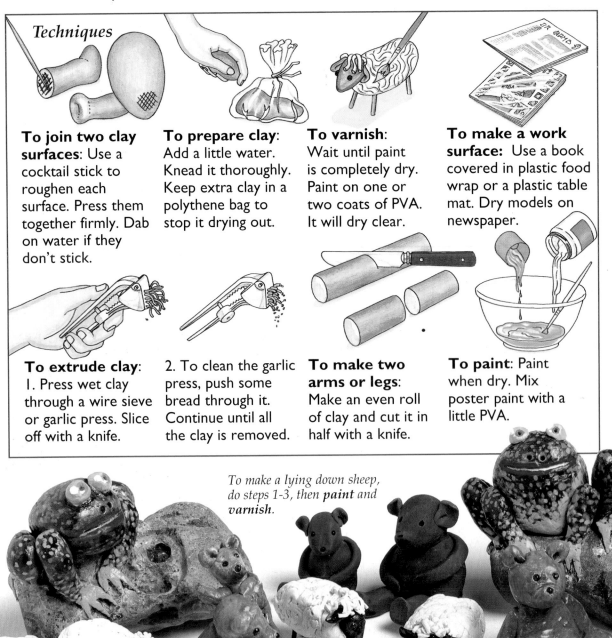

Techniques

To join two clay surfaces: Use a cocktail stick to roughen each surface. Press them together firmly. Dab on water if they don't stick.

To prepare clay: Add a little water. Knead it thoroughly. Keep extra clay in a polythene bag to stop it drying out.

To varnish: Wait until paint is completely dry. Paint on one or two coats of PVA. It will dry clear.

To make a work surface: Use a book covered in plastic food wrap or a plastic table mat. Dry models on newspaper.

To extrude clay: 1. Press wet clay through a wire sieve or garlic press. Slice off with a knife.

2. To clean the garlic press, push some bread through it. Continue until all the clay is removed.

To make two arms or legs: Make an even roll of clay and cut it in half with a knife.

To paint: Paint when dry. Mix poster paint with a little PVA.

*To make a lying down sheep, do steps 1-3, then **paint** and **varnish**.*

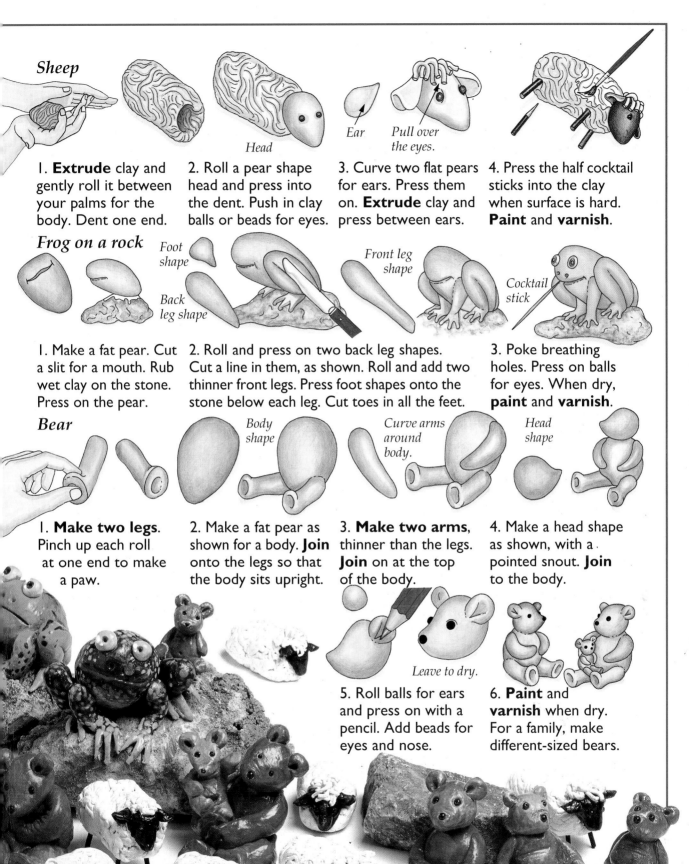

Sheep

1. **Extrude** clay and gently roll it between your palms for the body. Dent one end.

2. Roll a pear shape head and press into the dent. Push in clay balls or beads for eyes.

Head

3. Curve two flat pears for ears. Press them on. **Extrude** clay and press between ears.

Ear

Pull over the eyes.

4. Press the half cocktail sticks into the clay when surface is hard. **Paint** and **varnish**.

Frog on a rock

Foot shape

Back leg shape

Front leg shape

Cocktail stick

1. Make a fat pear. Cut a slit for a mouth. Rub wet clay on the stone. Press on the pear.

2. Roll and press on two back leg shapes. Cut a line in them, as shown. Roll and add two thinner front legs. Press foot shapes onto the stone below each leg. Cut toes in all the feet.

3. Poke breathing holes. Press on balls for eyes. When dry, **paint** and **varnish**.

Bear

Body shape

Curve arms around body.

Head shape

1. **Make two legs**. Pinch up each roll at one end to make a paw.

2. Make a fat pear as shown for a body. **Join** onto the legs so that the body sits upright.

3. **Make two arms**, thinner than the legs. **Join** on at the top of the body.

4. Make a head shape as shown, with a pointed snout. **Join** to the body.

Leave to dry.

5. Roll balls for ears and press on with a pencil. Add beads for eyes and nose.

6. **Paint** and **varnish** when dry. For a family, make different-sized bears.

Zoomer jet

This zoomer jet has a powerful launching action, so use it outside, away from other people. Paint it brightly so you can find it easily.

You will need:
tracing paper, soft pencil, sticky tape, ruler, paper clips, eraser, strong, thin cardboard (like a cereal box), strong glue (ask an adult for help), 6 small rubber bands, scissors, ballpoint pen, craft knife, cocktail stick, darning needle, felt-tip pens, PVA glue, 2 drawing pins.

Techniques
To trace:

1. Clip tracing paper over the patterns. Trace over the lines. Turn the tracing over and scribble over the lines with a soft pencil.

2. Turn your tracing back over and clip it onto cardboard. Draw firmly over the outlines again to transfer the patterns.

To score lines:

Lay a ruler along the line to be scored. Press firmly along the line with a ballpoint pen.

Cutting out

1. **Trace** the blue outline once and the red one twice onto cardboard.*
Cut out.

Don't cut dotted lines.

2. **Score** one fin along the dotted line. Turn the other over and **score**. Turn the jet over and **score** between aileron cuts.

Score here.

Score here.

3. Fold the fins up along the scored lines.

Decorate brightly.

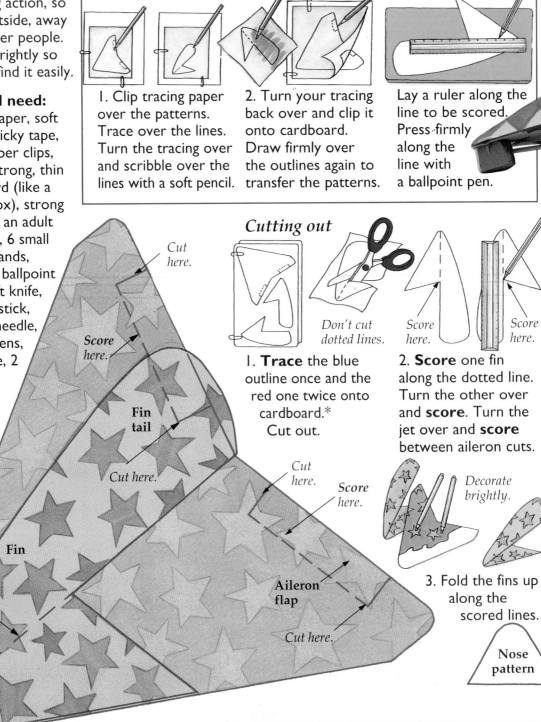

Jet pattern

Cut here.

Score here.

Fin tail

Cut here.

Fin

Score here.

Nose

Cut here.

Score here.

Aileron flap

Cut here.

Nose pattern

---

*If you use a cereal box, trace one of the red outlines onto the patterned side and one onto the grey side.

To launch the jet

1. Lay six rubber bands out in pairs. Pass one pair around the bottom end of a pencil and loop it through itself, as shown, pulling tightly.

2. Loop on the other pairs to make one long band. Pull tightly to knot.

3. Hold the launcher in one hand, hook the cocktail stick through the end of the bands, pull back very firmly, aim and release. *Cocktail stick*

Making up

Match edges.

Match middle lines.

For a jet spin, bend one aileron up and the other down.

1. Glue the folded-up fin pieces together. Glue them on the jet, lining up the middles.

2. Tape the fin tail to the jet on each side of the fin. Bend up the aileron flaps.

Make hole here.

Darning needle

Paper side of eraser.

3. **Trace** and cut out the nose pattern. Glue it onto a slice of eraser 1cm (½in) thick. When dry, cut around the nose shape with a craft knife. Turn it over.

4. Cut a 2cm (1in) piece of cocktail stick. Make a hole in the eraser with a darning needle.

5. Push the cocktail stick firmly into the hole. Remove, dip in glue and push it back into place. Leave to dry.

6. Glue the eraser to the nose with some strong glue. Glue the points of two drawing pins and press them into the eraser on either side of the fin.

5

Railway tunnel

This tunnel will fit a double or single track system (see patterns below), gauge H0/00 or smaller. You can see how to make it on the next four pages. It takes a while to make, but looks very realistic when it's finished.

You will need: adult-sized shoe box, at least 31 x 16 x 10cm, (12¼ x 6¼ x 4in), thin cardboard (such as a cereal box), tracing paper, pens, pencil, old scissors, ruler, PVA glue, 1 large sheet coarse sandpaper, 2 large sheets medium grade sandpaper, thin cardboard (black, grey or brown), ballpoint pen, sticky tape, poster paint (white, green, brown) old newspapers, paintbrushes (1 fine, 1 large), small stones.

Cutting out patterns

First, **trace the half pattern** you need from below. Glue onto thin cardboard and cut it out.

Place fold of tracing paper along straight edge.

Single track tunnel

Double track tunnel

6

Techniques

To trace half patterns: Clip folded tracing paper to the pattern and trace the lines. Turn the folded paper over and go over the lines again. Unfold to see the whole shape.

To dry-brush: Wipe most of the paint on your brush off onto newspaper, then brush over your model. It makes the cracks show up.

To score lines: page 4.

To make the tunnel (double track)

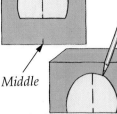

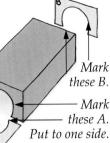

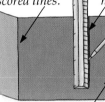

Middle

Mark these B.

Mark these A. Put to one side.

1. Mark both ends of your shoe box as shown. Match these marks with the fold on your pattern and draw around it.

2. Cut out the tunnel shapes from both ends. Stand the box on one end on the wrong side of coarse sandpaper and draw around it.

3. Cut out the shape you have drawn and mark it A. Mark A on the box end too. Repeat for the other end, marking with B.

Fold up along scored lines. *Score here.*

Use longer pieces here.

Box length

Use short pieces here.

1cm (³/₈in)

25cm (9 ⁷/₈in)

4. Cut thin, dark cardboard 49cm (19¼in) by the length of your box. **Score** two lines 12cm (4¾in) in from each end.

5. Push the shorter sides together so that the middle part curves up. Fit it inside the tunnel shape exactly and attach with tape.

6. Use old scissors to cut a strip of coarse sandpaper. Glue this inside the tunnel mouth, carefully matching the edges.

Single track

For the tunnel, use cardboard 47cm (18½in) wide by the box length. Use sandpaper 22 x 1cm (8⅝ x ³/₈in) for the inside. Make in the same way as the double track.

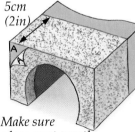

5cm (2in)

Make sure edges meet exactly.

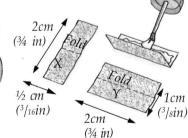

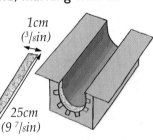

2cm (¾ in)

Fold X

½ cm (³/₁₆in)

2cm (¾ in)

Fold Y

1cm (³/₈in)

7. Cut and glue more sandpaper strips around the tunnel. Glue the sandpaper shapes from step 3 to each end, matching the As and the Bs.

8. Cut out two sizes of sandpaper bricks. Fold them in half, wrong sides together. Open out and put glue on wrong sides. Leave until glue is tacky.

9. Slide the X bricks around the tunnel arch, half in, half out. Press the Y bricks over the top edge, as shown. Glue on clusters of smaller bricks.

7

THIS MODEL CONTINUES OVER THE PAGE

To make the rock

1. Crumple small parcels of newspaper for rock. Pile them up over the tunnel, overlapping the edges of the sandpaper.

2. Use lots of glue to stick pieces of torn newspaper over the shape. This glues the rock to the tunnel.

3. Soak medium grade sandpaper in warm water for about 15 seconds. Squeeze it tightly. Open out and tear into large shapes.

Don't worry about lumps, they shrink.

4. Glue the shapes all over your newspaper. Brush over a mixture of glue and water. Put in a warm place to dry.

Plants and shrubs

You will need: PVA glue, sponge, cleaning sponge, thin cardboard, sieve, old comb, tea leaves, plastic food wrap, plasticine, twigs, paint, self-hardening clay, yogurt pot, blender.

Techniques
To make sponge mix:

1. Snip sponge carefully into a small blender, add a little water and switch on. Snip finely with scissors if you don't have a blender.

2. Press the water out in a fine sieve. Roll the sponge in paint. Use green and yellow for summer shrubs and red and yellow for autumn ones.

3. Mix up the sponge with glue until it is sticky. Use old yogurt pots, keeping different colours of sponge separate.

4. Put extra mix in a polythene bag to stop it drying out. Dry models on food wrap. They will peel off easily later.

Bushes

Glue different-sized small clumps of **sponge mix** onto your rock tunnel.

OR: Dry some moss on kitchen paper in a very cool oven. Glue onto the rock.

Shrubs

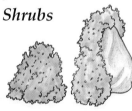

Make large clumps with **sponge mix** or press **sponge mix** over clay shapes. Leave to dry.

Timber

Cut thin twigs into 2cm (¾in) lengths. Glue together in a pile. Peel the twigs first if you like.

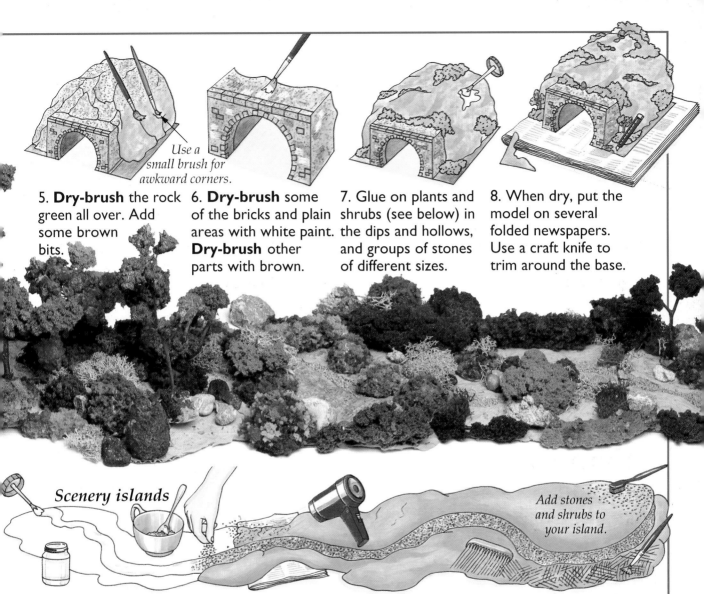

5. **Dry-brush** the rock green all over. Add some brown bits.

6. **Dry-brush** some of the bricks and plain areas with white paint. **Dry-brush** other parts with brown.

7. Glue on plants and shrubs (see below) in the dips and hollows, and groups of stones of different sizes.

8. When dry, put the model on several folded newspapers. Use a craft knife to trim around the base.

Use a small brush for awkward corners.

Scenery islands

Add stones and shrubs to your island.

1. Cut cardboard into one big island or lots of small ones to put by your railway. Paint paths on it with glue.

2. Grind up tea leaves and sprinkle them over the paths. Blow off extra with a hair dryer onto paper.

3. Roll green plasticine until very soft. Flatten and press it onto the cardboard, moulding it around the paths.

4. Pull a comb or old toothbrush over the plasticine to make it look like grass. **Dry-brush** dark green.

5. For trees, cut a twiggy branch 9 to 12cm (3½ to 4¾in) high. Set in a clay base and leave to dry.

6. Press different colours of **sponge mix** to the branches and over the base. Add more when dry.

7. For hedges, cut strips of cleaning sponge ½cm (¼in) wide. Paint with glue. Place on food wrap.

8. Stand the strips on edge and build them up with **sponge mix**. When they are dry, trim them to size.

9

Doll's tea party

You will need: craft knife, poster paint, thin fabric, cardboard egg box, toilet roll, margarine tub, PVA glue, plain flour, salt, cooking oil, 1egg, water, pen-top, spiky metal bottle cap, cocktail sticks **For set you also need**: thin cardboard, felt-tip pens, white paper, giftwrap, fine steel wire, scissors, stapler.

Table

A food can is a good guide.

1. Cut a circle from an egg box lid. Glue to a circle the same size cut from the lid of a margarine tub. Leave to dry.

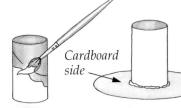

Cardboard side

2. Cut the toilet roll **to size** and **paint** white. When dry, glue to the middle of the circle.

3. Draw a circle around a small plate onto fabric and cut out. Wet the fabric and arrange it over the table top and base.

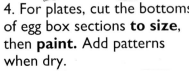

4. For plates, cut the bottoms of egg box sections **to size**, then **paint.** Add patterns when dry.

Techniques

To size models: Cut out rough table and plate shapes in paper to try out for size in your doll's house. Make them bigger or smaller if you need to and use as patterns.

To paint: Mix poster paint with a little glue for a smooth finish.

To glaze: Paint the surface of your food with whole beaten egg then bake at 180° C, 350°F (Gas mark 4) for 10-20 minutes (depending on size), until hard.

*You can also use large buttons with rims for plates. Rub down with fine sandpaper, then **paint**.*

Salt dough food

1. Mix 2 tablespoons of flour with 1 tablespoon of salt in a bowl. Add a drop of oil and some water. Knead it smooth.

Bottle cap

Dough rises, so make models smaller than you need.

2. Leave in a polythene bag in a freezer for an hour, or all night in the fridge. This amount makes a lot of food.

3. For a pie, roll a small ball of dough, flatten it slightly and press it in the cap. Remove any plastic first.

Press in with cocktail stick.

*When cool **paint** fruit red.*

4. Use a cocktail stick to prick out a circle. Mark the edge as shown. Cut out a slice with a craft knife.

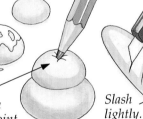

Press in with a pencil-point.

Slash lightly.

5. Roll a small ball for the top of the pie. Fill the empty slice with tiny balls for fruit. **Glaze** the pastry and bake.

6. Roll and shape dough into different loaves of bread. Dab on water with your finger to join shapes. **Glaze** and bake.

Tap sharply to release the scone.

For tiny scones, use a bendy straw. Blow the scones out.

7. For scones, dip a pen top into flour and press into thin patted-out dough. **Glaze** and bake.

8. When cool, draw jam around the scones with red felt-tip pen. Glue in a pile onto a plate.

Desk set

1. Roll giftwrap 2 x10cm (1 x 5in) tightly around a pencil. Glue. Slide off the pencil.

2. Cut out cardboard 1cm (½in) square. Cover with the same paper. Glue the end of the roll onto the square. Leave to dry.

3. For scissor handles, twist two pieces of wire around a cocktail stick. Cut to same size.

4. Cut thin cardboard 4 x ¼cm (1¾ x ⅛ in). Decorate to look like a ruler.

5. Cut cocktail sticks into 3cm and 4cm (1¼in and 1¾in) lengths. Colour with felt-tip pens.

6. Dip the ends of the ruler, scissors and pencils into glue. Arrange in the pot.

7. Cut rectangles of paper and giftwrap. Fold in half so the giftwrap is on the outside. Staple along fold. Glue on labels.

8. For a desk, make a table without a cloth.

Shipwrecked sailor

You will need:
big plastic or glass jar that you can get your hand inside (it must be clean and dry), thread, blue food dye, craft knife, plasticine, beads.

Techniques
To marble:

Roll together two or more balls of plasticine until streaky.
To extrude: Page 2.

The skeleton

Make all the parts separately then fit them all together inside the jar.
1. Roll and shape a white skull, press on grey balls for eye sockets, tiny beads for eyes, a triangular nose and a grinning mouth.
2. Roll tiny white teeth and press onto the mouth.
3. Roll a grey body. Press on a white spine and ribs.
4. Roll a grey ball and press on a white pelvis shape. Add to the main body.

5. For an arm or leg, roll a thin, white sausage. Loop and pinch the ends together. Pinch loop to another thin sausage. Do legs longer.
6. Press a pencil into triangle shapes to make hands and feet.
7. Press body into the jar first so it sits upright. Press on skull. Add arms, legs, hands and feet.

The background

Bend some pieces forward.

1. **Marble** balls of yellow and orange plasticine. Press them out over the base.

2. **Marble**, then roll, some thin, sausage shapes. Press in a clump against the back.

Sea bed

3. Add the skeleton. **Extrude** plasticine into strings. Pinch off and press in a clump.

4. Add shells, sponge, beads or coral and old jewellery for treasure. Press into the sea bed.

Snowstorm

You will need:
plasticine, I tube silver glitter, florists' wire, glycerine* (to slow glitter fall), food dye.

Make a model on the inside of a jar lid, no wider than the jar mouth. Keep checking that the lid will still screw on.

Press down firmly.

Twist wire for tree.

Fill jar in the sink, as the water will overflow when you put the lid on.

To make the snow

Add food dye if you like.

Water

Glycerine

1. Half fill the jar with glycerine. Add water until three quarters full. Add glitter.

2. Lower model inside. Liquid will rise to fill the jar. If not, add more water. Screw the lid on firmly.

3. Dry the jar, then carefully turn it the right way up and see the snow fall.

Fish and water

Press firmly into jar.

Add sharp teeth.

Use anything that water won't spoil such as foil, glass, beads, plastic toys and decorations. Press firmly into the plasticine.

1. Cut out fish shapes from flattened plasticine. Press on bright patterns.

2. For a hanging fish, **marble** and shape a fat fish and cut mouth.

Add blue food dye to water.

3. Tie a thread around the fish. Tie the other end around a lump of plasticine and press firmly inside the lid.

4. Pour water slowly to the top of the jar. Lower the hanging fish inside. Screw down the lid tightly.

*For one jam-jar, you will need at least 200ml (7 fl oz).

Look-again jokes

On these pages you'll find out how to make visual jokes to fool your friends and family.

You will need: craft knife, plastic modelling material (e.g. *Fimo®*), kitchen foil, waterbased gloss varnish, bendy straw, baking tray, 1 large round button, 1m (3ft) florists' stem wire, PVA glue, black thread, pipe cleaner, black poster paint or some black wool, plate.

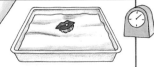

Techniques

To use plastic modelling material: Break off small pieces. Knead separately then join together. It is easier if you warm it first on a radiator.

To bake: Ask an adult to help you. Bake in the oven until hard, according to the instructions on the packet. Wait until it has cooled before you touch it.

Fun straws

Make sure the straw still fits in the hole.

1. For starlet lips, roll two fat, red sausages about 8cm (3in) long. Make them narrower at each end. Press together to make lips.

2. Pinch the top lip into a bow shape. Use the craft knife to make some pucker lines. Flatten the bottom lip a little in the middle.

3. Press the end of a bendy straw through the middle of the lips to punch a hole. Twist the straw around in the hole.

4. Put foil in the baking tray. Roll some more foil into a rounded pad about 1cm (½in) high. Curve the lips over the top. **Bake**.

Mix red with a little blue for a dark red.

Try making monster's lips in green or purple.

5. After the lips have cooled, varnish them to make them look glossy. When the varnish is completely dry, push a straw through the hole.

6. Use thinner sausages to make some dark red dracula lips. Miss out the puckers and add two long white fangs on either side of the hole.

Nail-through-head

Use old scissors. *Wind*

The wire should be hidden by your hair.

1. For the nail head, twist foil around a button, leaving a tail. Roll the tail up in a sheet of 28 x 28cm (11 x 11in) foil.

2. Twist and squeeze the foil into a long, firm, nail shape. Pinch the end into a point. Make sure the nail head is firmly attached.

3. Cut the nail in half. Attach one half to either end of a 35cm (13½in) length of wire. Wind the wire around the nail.

4. Paint the inner ends of the nail with red paint mixed with glue. When dry, bend the wire part around your head to fit.

Hairy scary spider

This hairy spider is easy to make and looks quite realistic. You could use it to scare anyone who doesn't like spiders.

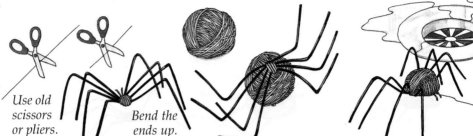

Use old scissors or pliers. *Bend the ends up.*

1. Cut a 36cm (14in) piece of wire into four by halving it, then halving again. Bind the pieces with black thread.

2. For the body, glue on a small ball of black wool, or a screwed-up piece of pipe cleaner, painted black.

3. Leave the spider in the bath, near the plughole. Tie on a long piece of fine black thread and tug it as someone comes near.

Fried egg

Make a flat, wavy circle from white **modelling material.** Flatten a ball of yellow onto it. **Bake** and varnish.

Ink blot

Splash some water on a plate. Copy the water shapes in blue or black modelling material to look like ink. **Bake.** Varnish so they look wet.

Castaway's raft

On the next four pages, you can see how to make this castaway's raft and some of the things he took with him from a desert island.
You will need: five garden canes 90cm (3ft) long OR peeled twigs (of even thickness), thick white cotton thread, 14 x 15cm (5½ x 6in) white or brown cotton fabric (from an old sheet), cup of strong cold tea, cereal box, potato, brown acrylic paint, plasticine, ruler, pencil, craft knife, scissors, sticky tape, darning needle, paintbrush, polystyrene packaging, varnish

Techniques
To cut cane:
1. Mark the length you want. Use a craft knife to saw around the cane. Avoid the knots in the cane, they are very hard.
2. Stand on the short end 2½cm (1in) from the cut. Pull the other end up sharply.
3. Trim ragged ends with scissors.
Knots: To stop knots untying, dab each one with a little varnish or clear nail polish.

To make the raft

Scatter a few dried bay leaves over the raft for banana leaves.

1. **Cut** two 15cm (6in) pieces of cane from the thinnest ends. Put aside. **Cut** twenty more 15cm (6in) canes.

2. Cut the top off the cereal box. Mark and cut a slit 8mm (¼in) wide on each side, down to 2½cm (1in) from the bottom.

3. Slot in a cane. Fold 1m (40in) of thread. Wind it twice around one end as shown. Tie a double **knot**. Repeat for the other end.

Middle of thread

Strut

Knot here

Needle

4. Slot in a second cane. Tie on with double **knots**. Add the other eighteen canes in the same way. Remove from box.

5. Tape on two 18cm (7½in) canes over the threads. Wrap doubled thread in a figure of eight around the ends as shown. **Knot**.

6. Remove tape. Sew the threads between the middle two canes to the strut below as shown. **Knot**. Repeat on the other side.

Plasticine

Glue here so they don't slip down the mast.

Keep the tea.

7. Repeat step 6 for the threads between struts 5 and 6 and 15 and 16 on both sides of the raft. These are shown in red above.

8. Cut a 20cm (8in) cane for the mast. Shave the thin end. Push firmly between the middle two canes. Wedge upright.

9. Tie thread to one corner. Wind it around the mast 2cm (¾in) from the top. **Knot**. Repeat for the other corners. Glue as shown.

10. Dip the sail cotton in tea until coloured. Leave to dry. Cut a design on half the potato. Dip it in paint and press onto the sail.

Tape on under ropes.

11. Wrap each end of the sail around the two canes you put aside. Sew on with big stitches. Cut a slit in the top of the mast.

12. Tape on the sail along the line of the canes. Tie thread to one end and pull it through the slit. Tie at the other end.

13. Take off the tape. Tie threads from the bottom of the sail to the back corners. Paint all the threads with cold tea.

14. Try your raft in the water. If it is too low, put polystyrene underneath to help it float. The raft will keep it in place.

17

THIS MODEL CONTINUES OVER THE PAGE

Raft extras

You will need: kitchen roll tube, bread knife, thin cardboard (cereal box), silver takeaway food carton lid, masking tape, kitchen foil, PVA glue, poster or acrylic paint, wooden cheesebox or 1 garden cane, fabric, bayleaves, old flat shoelace, hole-punch, hammer, nail, fine string or strong thread, plasticine, twig, cold tea, hazelnuts, sandpaper, walnut, felt-tip pens, plastic modelling material (e.g. *Fimo* ®), cocktail stick

Techniques	To use plastic modelling
To score: page 4	**material:** page 14
To paint: page 2	**To bake:** page 14

Treasure chest

Bread knife

1. For the lid, cut a piece of kitchen roll tube 4cm (1½in) long. Draw around one end onto thin cardboard. Cut out and cut in half.

Use creases as a guide.

Masking tape

2. Press the roll lightly to flatten. Cut in half lengthways. Re-shape one half. Stick a semicircle onto each end of the half roll.

3. For the box, draw around the base of the lid onto the middle of your cereal box. Add four side pieces 2cm (¾in) deep as shown.

2cm (¾ in)

4. **Score** the red lines. Cut out the shape and turn it over. Turn up the flaps to make the box sides. Secure with tape.

Put tape on inside.

Don't worry about wrinkles in the foil.

5. Glue and press kitchen foil all over the lid and base, shiny side out. Attach the lid with masking tape, along one long edge.

6. **Paint** the outside dark brown for a beaten look. Let some silver show through. When dry, pad inside with crumpled foil.

7. Punch holes in silver carton lid for coins. Use shiny beads, old jewellery, bits of chain and doll's house cutlery for treasure.

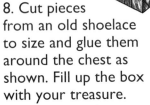

8. Cut pieces from an old shoelace to size and glue them around the chest as shown. Fill up the box with your treasure.

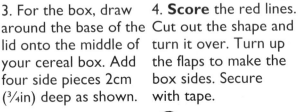

You can use plasticine instead of hazelnuts.

For exotic vegetables and fruit, dry flower seed heads, or small pods or petals.

Treasure raft

Ask an adult to help you make this.

Craft knife

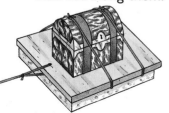

Plasticine

1. Measure and draw out a 7 x 8cm (2¾ x 3in) rectangle on a wooden lid. Place a ruler by each line then cut along them.

2. Make a hole with a hammer and nail in the front of the raft. Thread fine string through the hole and tie it in a loop.

3. Cut the string long enough to attach to the big raft. Tie the treasure chest on as shown. Add a float if you want to.

OR: Cut cane 7cm (2¾in) long to make a small raft like the one on page 16. Tie string around a cane on each raft to join them.

Odds and ends

1. For a water jar, mix red and green plasticine to make brown. Roll a ball and flatten lightly on top.

2. Press on another small ball and push in a blunt pencil to make a dent with a lip. Peel a twig and cut to size. Add to the jar for a cork.

3. Dip string into cold tea. Coil into a rope while still wet. When dry, unravel the ends slightly.

4. Cut a square of the same fabric as the sail and fold it into a parcel. Tie the folded fabric with fine string. Dip it into cold tea.

5. For coconuts, rub hazelnuts with sandpaper or a cheese grater. Make three black dots with a felt-tip pen.

6. Model fruit from **plastic modelling material**. Roll oranges on sandpaper. **Bake**. Add markings when cool.

7. For a basket, carefully push open the halves of a walnut with a blunt knife. This is quite tricky. Scoop out the nut and fill with your fruit.

8. For a harpoon, cut off one tip of a cocktail stick. Colour the rest with a brown felt-tip pen. Model plasticine fish and thread them on.

9. For a parrot, press bright colours of plasticine into a long bullet shape. Pinch head and tail shapes. Mark wings with a knife.

10. Add eyes and a beak. For feet, press two small plasticine rolls onto the top of the mast. Press your parrot onto the feet.

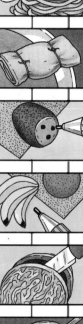

Models you can eat

You can make these models just for fun or for birthday cakes. Make all the parts and put them together at the last minute. Always make jellies the day before you need them.

You will need: 2 packets ready-roll white icing, 2 green jellies, round tray, sponge cake (bought or made), blue and red food dye, jam, non-toxic black paint (for eyes), kitchen foil, plastic food wrap, caster sugar, icing sugar, sieve, rolling pin, knife, pastry brush.
For the brown bear, you also need: yellow and green food dye, chocolate powder.

Preparation and techniques

To make up the jellies: Follow the packet instructions to make two bowls of jelly. Add blue food dye to one bowl for a darker green.
To cover the tray: Cover a tray with kitchen foil, then with food wrap. This stops the jelly tasting of the foil.
To make bears: page 2
To marble: page 12
To extrude: page 2

Icebergs, sea and bears

Cover completely.

This part is tricky.

Ball of icing

1. Cut the cake into large, uneven chunks. Pile them up in the shape of an iceberg on one side of the tray. Stick them in place with a little jam.

2. Make two or three small icebergs using single pieces of cake. Use the pastry brush to paint them with jam mixed with a little hot water.

3. Sift icing sugar over the work surface and rolling pin. Roll out the icing ½cm (¼in) thick. Lift up as shown and unroll over the piled-up cake.

4. Press the icing to the cake with a ball of icing. Trim all around. Cover the other shapes in the same way.

Make different sized bears.

5. **Make two bears** with the icing. Sprinkle caster sugar over the icebergs for glittery snow. Stick the bears on with a little water.

6. Cut your jellies up with a knife. Spoon the light green jelly around the icebergs. Fill up the spaces with the dark green jelly.

Brown bear cake

1. Pile up plain or chocolate sponge rocks on the tray. Cover with icing as for the iceberg. Paint brown (mix red, yellow and green food dye). When dry, rub in chocolate powder.

2. **Extrude** green icing for grass. **Make bears** from icing. Paint brown with food dye. Put on rocks. Add icing flowers if you like.

For a special dessert, use white ice cream cut into blocks instead of cake and icing.

Seal

Flipper

Use a few drops only.

1. Mix red and blue food dye together to make icing purple. Roll it into a long pear shape.

2. Cut a tail. Add and mark flippers as shown. Flatten two balls and press on for cheeks. Add a tiny nose.

Fish

Poke in tiny icing balls for eyes.

3. **Marble** purplish -grey icing and blue icing. Make fish shapes, cutting the mouth and tail with a knife. Mark on scales. Add eyes.

21

Wizard

Making the wizard

Head

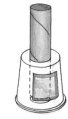
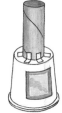
Body

You will need: egg (size 2 or 3), darning needle, kitchen roll, long cardboard tube, 11 pipe cleaners 15cm (6in) long, yogurt pot, masking tape, felt-tip pen, craft knife, scissors, ruler, thin cotton fabric, glue mix (²/₃ PVA, ¹/₃ water), small household paintbrush, wool, washable tray, plastic food wrap, hard book, poster paints, decorations.

1. **Blow an egg.** Bend a pipe cleaner in half and tape it to the egg as shown. Leave a tail for the neck.

2. Cut a cardboard tube to 19cm (17½in). Place on a yogurt pot base. Draw around it and cut out the shape.

3. Push the tube inside, almost to base level. Make sure it is upright. Tape firmly in place.

Cut open here.

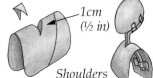
1cm (½ in)
Shoulders
Thumbs point up.

4. Lightly flatten a bit of tube 6cm (2½in) long. Round off the lower corners. Cut the bottom edge.

5. Snip a V-shape in the middle of the top edge. Push in the pipe cleaner and bend. Tape inside, leaving a neck.

6. Twist together five pipe cleaners. Bend one end up for a thumb. Repeat for other arm. Tape inside shoulders.

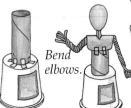
Bend elbows.
Tray
Wrinkles will add to the effect.

7. Lightly flatten the top of the tube. Place the shoulders over the top. Tape in place. Bend the arms down at the shoulders.

8. Brush glue mix onto kitchen roll strips 2½cm (1in) wide. Cover the head. Mould a hooked nose and press on.

Leave thumbs free.
Mould hands.

9. Wind glued strips of kitchen roll around the neck and onto the shoulders. Wind more strips from the elbows to the hands.

10. Add another layer of strips. Mould the ends into a hand shape. Put the figure on plastic food wrap. Paint when dry.

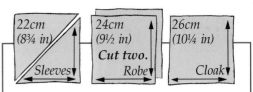

22cm (8¾ in)	24cm (9½ in) **Cut two.**	26cm (10¼ in)
Sleeves↙	Robe↓	Cloak↓

Arrange the arms, hands, head and folds before the fabric dries.

Dressing the figure

1. **Colour** your glue mix if you like. Cut fabric to the sizes shown above. Dip fabric in water and squeeze out. Spread on the tray and brush with lots of glue mix.

2. Gather the edge of one robe. Smooth onto the back of the shoulders, glue side out. Repeat at the front. Overlap fabric at the sides.

3. Fold back 1cm (½in) of long edge of sleeves. Cut off the small triangles. Drape over arms as shown. Press edges together underneath.

4. Place two corners of the cloak around the neck so they meet in front. Arrange it in drapes. Turn back the sides over the shoulders.

5. **Make a cone**. Glue it onto the head. When dry, **paint** with glue mix.

6. Dip wool strands in some uncoloured glue mix. Press on for a beard and hair. Press on a long moustache. Allow to dry.

7. Wrap a strip of glued kitchen roll around hat to cover ends of hair. Paint when dry if you like.

Add a cocktail stick for a wand.

Add sequins, glitter, bits of old jewellery, small glass beads, or silver or gold braid. Twisted kitchen foil makes good jewellery.

Make smaller figures by using a walnut for the head and a toilet roll tube for the body.

Indoor garden

Techniques

To make frogs: page 3

To make a bird: page 19

To make trees and bushes: page 8

To marble: page 12

If you keep this living garden watered and out of direct sunlight, it will last for quite a long time.

You will need: waterproof plastic tray, 2 plastic tub lids (1 white, 1 round), peat or bulb fibre, felt-tip pen, moss, artificial flowers, low-growing rockery plants, tiny stones or gravel, different sized and coloured larger stones, water, PVA glue, poster paint, paintbrush, plasticine, thimbles, tissue paper, sponge mix (see page 8), heather, sticky tape, kitchen foil. You can add lots of your own bits and pieces. Don't add anything that will be spoiled by water.

Make bushes or press real heather into peat.

Make a tree. Press into plasticine.

To lay out your garden

Back left

Felt-tip pen

Lid

Front left

1. Draw a winding path on your tray, with a wider area in the back left corner. Add the upturned round lid for a pond.

2. Fill in around the path and lid with a layer of peat or bulb fibre. Build it up higher in the front left corner.

Press real plants into peat between clumps of moss.

Grow cress from seed on the peat, or cut a section from some bought from a supermarket.

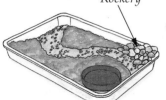

Rockery

3. Fill the path with tiny stones. Pile up larger stones in the back right corner for a rockery. Press peat between the stones.

4. Cover the peat with clumps of moss. Water along the path and around the edges. Add tiny plants to the rockery.

The pond

1. Take the lid from the tray. Cover it with crumpled foil. Paint with a mix of glue and blue paint. Add green and paint again.

2. Push in little stones around the outside. Cover the edges with moss. Add some artificial flowers if you like.

Model a cat like this. Paint on stripes.

Garden trellis

½ cm (¼ in)
1½ cm (½ in)

1. Cut two rectangles 6 x 8cm (2½ x 3in) from the white lid. Cut out the middles. Leave a border.

2. Cut strips of thin, white cardboard ½cm (¼in) wide and glue in a criss-cross pattern on the back.

3. Hinge the two pieces together at the back with sticky tape. Stand in the back left corner.

Marble two colours of plasticine together. Model a bird bath like this.

Make birds and press on around the rim. Fill the bowl with real water.

Make some frogs. Just make the heads and show them peeping out of the moss.

Cut several butterfly shapes at once from layers of folded tissue paper. Scatter on the moss.

Fill thimbles or flower tubs made from plasticine with peat. Press in tiny dried or artificial flowers.

Model a duck out of plasticine. Add to the pond.

Wiggling eel

The mechanism for this eel is quite tricky, but it makes a great wiggly effect.

You will need: small empty drink carton with narrow straw at least 106mm (4in) long, craft knife, scissors, ruler, pliers, ballpoint pen, darning needle, sticky tape, coloured plastic bag, stiff paper, PVA glue, 2 lengths of florists' wire 23cm (9in) and 1 length 30cm (12in) - you can join 2 x 18cm (7in) pieces together by overlapping ends 2½cm (1in) and twisting together.

Techniques

To make holes: Push a darning needle through the carton and wiggle it around to widen the hole.
To bend wire: Hold the wire firmly and bend sharply down.
To cut wire: Use pliers with a wirecutting edge, or old scissors.

Make sure the holes are big enough.

Check that the mechanism isn't rubbing on the side of the box. Pull the box wider if it is.

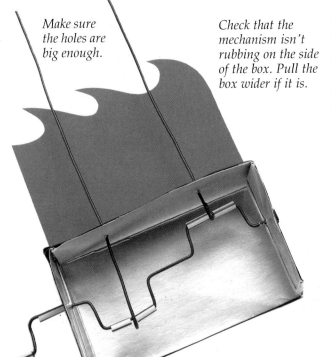

To make the mechanism

Midpoint · *Slit*

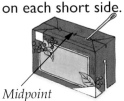

Midpoint

1. Cut off one long side of the carton and stand it on those edges. Mark the midpoint at the top on each short side.

2. Draw a dot 2½cm (1in) down from each mark. **Make a hole** on each dot. Cut a slit from the bottom of each side to the holes.

3. Draw a line along the middle of the top. Mark the midpoint with a dot. **Make holes** 2½cm (1in) to each side of this dot.

4. Cut 2 pieces of straw 2¼cm (⅞in) long. Cut each in half to make 4 short straws. Cut another piece 2½cm (1in) long.

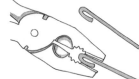

1¼ cm (½ in) · *Middle*

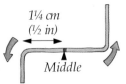

5. Make a ½cm (¼in) loop in one end of each short wire. Nip the ends together with pliers to close the loop. Put aside.

6. Find the middle of the long wire. Go 1¼cm (½in) to each side. **Bend** the left side down and the right side up.

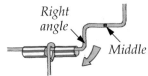

Right angle · *Middle*

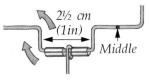

2½ cm (1in) · *Middle*

7. Go 1½cm (½in) down from the left corner. **Bend** it out at right angles. Thread on a short straw, then the loop of a short wire, then a short straw.

8. **Bend** up the wire 2½cm (1in) along from the last corner. Go 1½cm (½in) up the wire and **bend** it out again at right angles.

Cut other models from paper and colour them in. Tape to the wires.

To make the eel

To make the eel

1. Cut a strip 25 x 2½cm (10 x 1in) from the plastic bag. Cut a head and tail and mark an eye on each side.

2. Tape the wires to the back, 2½cm (1in) from the head and 13cm (5in) from the tail. Turn the handle to see it lash its tail.

Middle

Hole

B   A

Middle

Make sure wires can move freely.

9. Flip the wires over so it looks like A. Repeat steps 7 - 8 so that the whole thing looks like picture B.

10. Turn the box upside down. Drop the free ends of the wires into the box and through the holes.

11. Feed the ends of the long wire up the slits to the holes. Put some tape along each slit to hold the wire.

12.* Pull the top left wire gently upward. **Cut** the side left wire to 2½cm (1in) then make a loop.

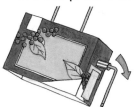

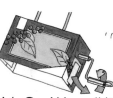

13. **Cut** the side right wire to 6½cm (2½in). Cut and thread on a 1½cm (½in) straw. **Bend** wire down 1½cm (½in) from the box.

14. Go 1½cm (½in) down this wire and **bend** it out. Thread on the long piece of straw. Make a loop in the end of the wire so it won't come off.

15. Turn the model upside down and shake it gently. Put it the right way up and pull the handle gently away from the box as you turn it.

16. To decorate the box, cut stiff paper into wave shapes. Stick onto the sides of the box. Add seaweed and fish. Make an eel and add to the wires (see above).

27

If you are left-handed, do step 12 to the right side wire and steps 13 and 14 to the left side wire.

Castle of doom

On the next four pages, you can see how to make this dramatic scene. Use it to display your knights, or as an arena for *Dungeons and Dragons ®* games. It takes a while to make, but you can work on several parts at once.

The list below tells you what you need to make a castle like the one in the picture, but you can add your own spooky features. The techniques you need are listed on this page.

You will need: cardboard from a strong box, sticky tape, wide masking tape, poster paints, dark grey ready-mix paint, PVA glue, newspaper, medium grade sandpaper, kitchen foil, egg boxes, white and red tissue paper, craft knife, scissors, lkg and ½kg (2lb and 1lb) margarine tubs, self-hardening clay, cocktail sticks, small plastic or cardboard container, round food tin, toilet rolls, kitchen roll and tubes, plastic drinks' bottles, thin cardboard, florists' wire, large plastic handles (from washing detergent or drinks' containers), sponge, thin twigs.

Techniques

To dry-brush: page 6
To make rock: page 8, steps 1-4
To make a bear: page 3
To extrude: page 2
To make cones: page 18
To paint: page 2
To make trees and shrubs: page 8

This will fit on a desk-top in your room. Place a reading lamp to the side or behind for an extra-spooky effect.

The background

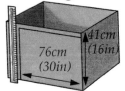

1. For the base, cut strong cardboard as shown. Use wide masking tape if you need to join pieces.

76cm (30in) × 41cm (16in)

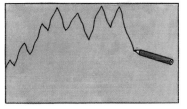

2. For the background, draw jagged mountain peaks on cardboard, 132 x 41cm (52 x 16in).

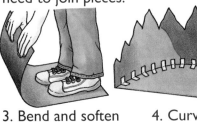

Trim off extra base and tape at the back.

3. Bend and soften the background as shown. It will crease. Cut out the mountains.

4. Curve them between two corners of the base. Tape on. **Paint** dark grey.

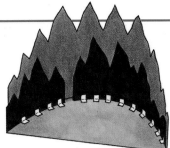

5. Draw and cut out more mountains from softened cardboard. **Paint** black. Tape on in front of the others.

Stick on shiny side down

6. For the castle rock, tape four egg boxes together. Tape to the base in front of the mountains.

7. **Make rock** over the boxes. Leave the top flat and make the sides rugged. **Dry-brush** light grey.

8. For the river, paste the shiny side of some kitchen foil. Press it to the base so it goes behind the rock.

9. Paste the top and press on pieces of white tissue over it. **Dry-brush** white when dry.

10. **Make rock** for a bank, overlapping the edge of the foil river. **Dry-brush** rock dark grey.

For a spooky red light, cover the end of a small torch with red tissue paper. Cut a hole in the background cardboard and push the torch through.

Old metal jewellery can make a building look scary.

CONTINUED OVER THE PAGE

The pit

1. Draw around a small container on the base of a ½kg margarine tub.

2. Cut out the shape. Press in the container for a pit. Tape in place.

3. **Make rock** over tub. Leave the pit open. **Dry-brush** dark grey.

4. Paste kitchen roll and press it inside the pit with a brush.

5. Crumple extra paper around the rim. **Paint** the inside black.

6. Paste red tissue. Crumple it inside for a fire pit. Drop in red and black clay coals.

OR: **Make a bear** from clay. **Paint** it brown and place in the pit. Add some small clay bones.

OR: **Extrude** clay strands for snakes. Press onto pit and **paint** brightly.

29

The castle

1. Cut cartons, tubes, and plastic bottles to different heights for towers and turrets. Arrange on the rock, but don't stick on yet.

2. Place a round turret piece a quarter over the corner of a square tower piece. Draw carefully around the shape.

²/₃ height of turret

3. Cut around the line, then down each side. Cut in from the corner on both sides and remove. Tape the turret in place.

Cut with a craft knife.

4. Cut handles from large plastic containers as shown. Tape handle between two towers to make a flying buttress.

Detergent container

Don't worry about the wrinkles. They add to the effect.

5. Glue kitchen roll all over the towers. When dry, **paint** mid-grey. **Dry-brush** white. Paint on doors and narrow windows.

6. **Make cones** for roofs. Cover with kitchen foil (shiny side down). **Paint** black. Some foil will show through.

7. Cut wire flagpoles. Wrap torn tissue around them for flags and **paint** black. Poke the flagpoles into the roofs and tape inside.

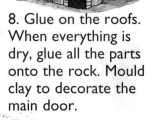

8. Glue on the roofs. When everything is dry, glue all the parts onto the rock. Mould clay to decorate the main door.

The cave of skulls

1. Cut a doorway in the side of a large tub, big enough for your figures. Tape in place.

Leave door open.

2. **Make rock** over the top, sides and base, but not the front. **Dry-brush** dark grey.

Press in nose and eyes.

Press pencil in eyes.

3. **Model** two clay steps. Press a half-skull shape above the door, like this.

4. Add fangs down the sides, jagged teeth, and eyeballs. **Paint** when dry.

5. Cut cocktail sticks to different lengths. Mould tiny skulls on top. **Paint** when dry.

6. Stack flattened clay balls on either side of the doorway. Press the sticks into them.

Finishing touches

Steps
Skulls
Bridge
Ladder

1. Cut a plastic handle large enough to fit over the river. Tape it in place for a bridge.

2. Glue kitchen roll all over it, covering the tape. **Paint** light grey. **Dry-brush** dark grey.

3. Add clay steps up to the bridge and castle. Add skulls on either side.

4. Glue on grey **shrubs and trees**. **Dry-brush** trunks white. Push into clay rocks. Add clay boulders by the river.

5. Paste crumpled kitchen roll all over the base, covering the front edge. **Paint** light grey. **Dry-brush** a darker colour.

6. For a ladder, cut two thin twigs to size. Glue on the top and bottom rungs. When dry, add the other rungs and **paint**. Miss out a few rungs.

31

Tools and materials

You can use the techniques in this book to make up your own exciting models. Try making a nativity scene with figures made like the wizard on page 22, and the sheep on page 2. Or, make a haunted house like the castle of doom on page 28. Look out for interestingly shaped boxes and cartons that you can use in your models. Some basic model-making tools and materials are shown below.

Stockists
You will find most of the tools and materials you need in large stationers' or craft shops. You can buy stem wire from florists' shops, sandpaper from hardware stores, cane from garden centres, ready-roll icing and cocktail sticks from food shops and glycerine from a chemist.

Essentials
craft knife, scissors, paintbrushes, felt-tip pens, ballpoint pens, pencils, poster paint, PVA glue, sticky tape, ruler

Things to collect
tissue paper, plastic food wrap, sponge, kitchen foil, cardboard tubes, egg boxes, drinks cartons, margarine tubs, newspapers, cocktail sticks, drawing pins, pipe cleaners, old jewellery, beads, straws

Useful materials and equipment

self-hardening clay, plasticine, plastic modelling material, florists' stem wire, thin cardboard, coloured stiff paper, tracing paper, sandpaper, ready-roll icing, food dye, glitter, masking tape, thread, cotton fabric, garlic press, pliers

First published in 1994 by Usborne Publishing Ltd., Usborne House, 83-85 Saffron Hill, London EC1N 8RT, England. Copyright © 1994 Usborne Publishing Ltd. The name Usborne and the device ♨ are Trade Marks of Usborne Publishing Ltd. All rights reserved.